It's Bedtime

Lil' Marco

IT'S BEDTIME LIL' MARCO
Published by Frog Pond Publishing
P.O. Box 452721
Garland, TX 75045-2721
Hardcover ISBN-13: 978-1-7326867-6-2
         ISBN-10: 1-7326867-6-9

Edited by Ann Fields
Published in the United States by Coffee Creek Media Group.

It's Bedtime
Lil' Marco

This book is dedicated to:

_____

This is Lil' Marco.
Lil' Marco likes the backyard.
Lil' Marco likes to run and play.

It's time to come inside,
said Lil' Marco's daddy.
It's almost bedtime, Lil' Marco!

5

Daddy. Daddy, cried Lil' Marco!
Lil' Marco wants to play basketball.

It's bedtime, Lil' Marco!
Daddy. Daddy.
Lil' Marco wants his red truck.

It's bedtime, Lil' Marco!
Daddy. Daddy.
Lil' Marco wants to stay outside.

It's bedtime, Lil' Marco!
Daddy. Daddy.
Lil' Marco wants to take a bath.

9

It's bedtime, Lil' Marco!
Daddy. Daddy.
Lil' Marco wants to blow bubbles in the tub.

It's bedtime, Lil' Marco!
Daddy. Daddy.
Lil' Marco wants to read his book.

It's bedtime, Lil' Marco!
Daddy. Daddy.
Lil' Marco wants to play with his teddy bear.

It's bedtime, Lil' Marco!
Daddy.
Lil' Marco wants to jump on the bed.

13

It's bedtime, Lil' Marco!
Daddy.
Lil' Marco wants his little blue blanket.

14

It's bedtime, Lil' Marco!
Daddy.
Lil' Marco wants to play hide and seek.

15

It's bedtime, Lil' Marco!
Dad.
Lil' Marco wants a hug and a kiss.

It's bedtime, Lil' Marco!
Dad.
Lil' Marco wants to be covered up.

17

It's bedtime, Lil' Marco!
Dad.
Lil' Marco wants his night light on.